Two for the Show

STARRING JIM HENSON'S MUPPETS™

By Horace B.T. Calhoun

Illustrated by Sue Venning

To Tuck and Dude
—S.V.

6/88
Amer media
#10.89

Copyright © 1982, 1986 by Henson Associates, Inc.
THE MUPPET SHOW, MUPPET, and MUPPET character names are trademarks of Henson Associates, Inc.
All rights reserved under International and Pan-American Copyright Conventions.
Published in the U.S.A. by Western Publishing Company, Inc.
in conjunction with Henson Associates, Inc. and adapted from a Random House book.

GOLDEN® & GOLDEN & DESIGN® are trademarks of Western Publishing Company, Inc.

Library of Congress Cataloging in Publication Data: Calhoun, Horace B.T. Two for the show. SUMMARY: Robin and
Sweetums, respectively too small and too big to be on the Muppet show, start their own fixing business. [1. Size and
shape—Fiction] I. Henson, Jim. II. Venning, Sue, ill. III. Title PZ7.C12775 Tw [E] 82-3725 AACR2
ISBN 0-307-13978-6
Manufactured in the United States of America 1 2 3 4 5 6 7 8 9 0

Robin, Kermit the Frog's little nephew, walked up to the backstage bulletin board and read the list of acts for that night's *Muppet Show*.

"Maybe my name will be on the list today." He crossed his flippers for luck. But no, his name wasn't on the list. Robin sighed. He wanted more than anything to be on the *Muppet Show*.

Just then Sweetums walked up. He read the list of acts carefully.

"You're not in the show tonight either, are you, Sweetums?" Robin said.

"No. Kermit says I'm too big to be in the show."

"And he tells me I'm too small," said Robin.

"I wish he'd change his mind," they said together.

BULLETIN BOARD

2. Fix hole in armadillo's dressing room wall.

THINGS TO DO RIGHT AWAY:
1. Walk armadillo

hen Robin had an idea. "Even though
e not in the show, we can still help
." He looked at Kermit's list of
IGS TO DO RIGHT AWAY. "How about
walk the armadillo while you fix
hole?"

t's a deal," Sweetums agreed.
Robin grabbed Andy the
adillo's leash, and
etums found a tool kit.
n they headed toward the
t star's
sing room.

Robin knocked and then opened the door. "Hello? Mr. Armadillo? We're here to take you for a walk."

"And to fix the hole in your wall."

Andy the bouncing Armadillo said nothing. But the minute his leash was on, he started to bounce. He bounced off the wall. He bounced off the ceiling. He made holes all over the room with his hard armadillo shell.

And Robin bounced with him because he was too small to do anything about it.

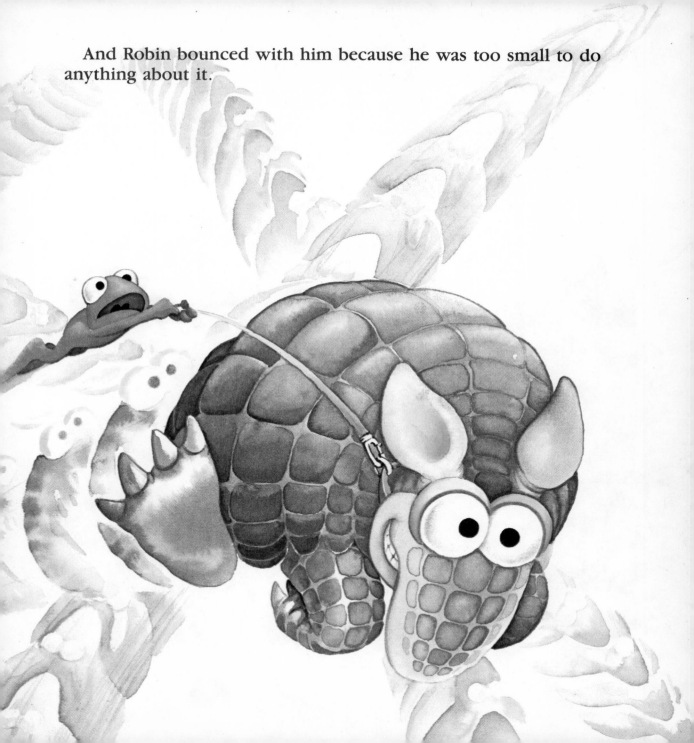

Sweetums stood there with his hammer and nails. Andy was making so many holes that Sweetums didn't know which one to fix first.

Then, BERROING! CRASH! Andy bounced his biggest bounce yet. He got stuck in the ceiling. "I guess this is one way to walk an armadillo," said Robin, dangling from the leash far above the floor.

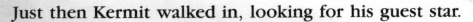

Just then Kermit walked in, looking for his guest star.

"I was just taking Andy for a walk."

"And that's how you turned a perfectly good dressing room into Swiss cheese?"

"Yes! Now that you mention it..." said Robin.

'I don't believe this,'' moaned Kermit.

"Rehearsals for the show start in an hour. See if you two can have this room fixed up by then."

"Right, boss," said Sweetums. He helped Robin down and pulled Andy out of the ceiling.

"Don't worry, Uncle Kermit, we'll clean it up," Robin promised.

Sweetums and Robin got to work. First they tied Andy down so he couldn't bounce into any more trouble.

Then Sweetums fixed the holes while Robin swept the floor. "There!" Sweetums banged in the last nail. "All done!"

The room looked great.

"You know, Sweetums, we might not be the right size for the show, but we sure can fix things," Robin said thoughtfully. "In fact, we're so good at it, why don't we forget the show **and go into the** fixing business?"

"Good idea! I like fixing things."

So the two friends made a big sign and hung it up in the alley behind the theater.

In no time there were all sorts of jobs for Robin and Sweetums to do.

First they papered Rizzo's rat hol

Then they helped Beauregard paint scenery.

Then they rescued Foo-Foo from under a parked car.

Then they dusted Miss Piggy's chandelier.

Their new business was a success!

Meanwhile, inside the theater, Kermit was directing rehearsals for the big finale, "Jack and the Beanstalk."

Fozzie Bear played the giant. He wore stilts but wasn't too good at balancing.

Andy the Armadillo played Jack. He was really good at bouncing.

Suddenly Andy bounced right into Fozzie. Fozzie fell and grabbed the beanstalk. I fell down from the rafters and landed right on top of Andy. Andy loved it. He bounced higher and higher!

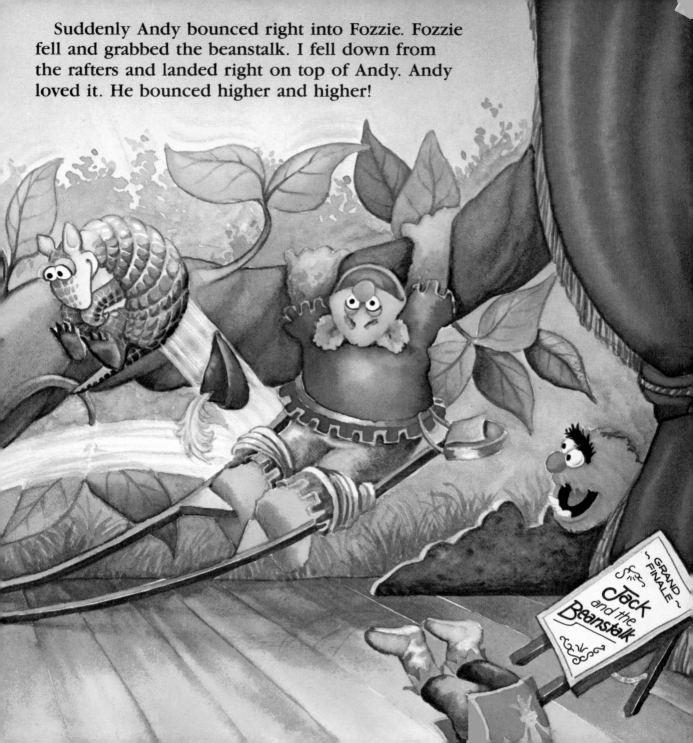

"Stop!" Kermit shouted. No one stopped! "Andy! You're FIRED!" As Andy bounced happily down the street, making large holes in the sidewalk, Kermit noticed Robin and Sweetums' sign.

"No job too big or too small," he read. "Hmmm, that gives me an idea."

Robin & Sweetums
If you're in a fix,
call us.
No job too BIG
or too small

Robin and Sweetums had just finished fixing Pops' antique back scratcher.

"Hey, you guys," said Kermit. "Can you do a job for me?"

"Sure, Uncle Kermit. Is it a big job or a small one?"

"Both! Follow me."

OFFICE

Kermit led Robin and Sweetums to the costume room. Holding out two costumes, he said, "Here. Put these on."

"But, Uncle Kermit, I don't understand."

"It's part of the job," explained Kermit.

So Sweetums and Robin put on the costumes.

Then Kermit led them backstage. "Okay, Sweetums, repeat after me: Fee, fi, fo, fum."

"Fee, fi, fo, fum."

"Uncle Kermit!" Robin interrupted. "Please tell us what the job is. We have lots of customers waiting."

"Well...the job is to star in the final number for tonight's show."

WHAT?"

We're doing 'Jack and the Beanstalk', "
tinued Kermit. " Someone small has to be Jack,
someone big has to be the giant. You two are
right. I don't know why I didn't think of it
ore."

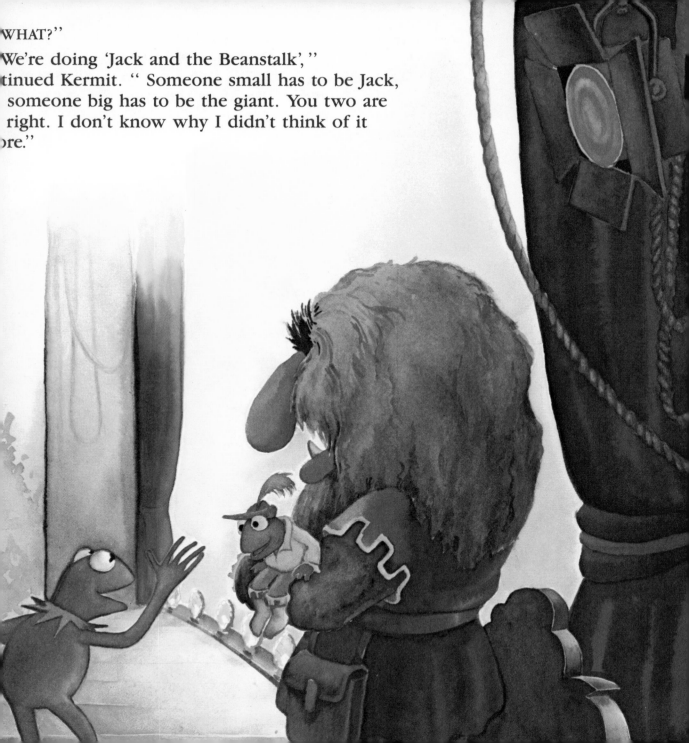

So that night Robin and Sweetums starred in the show. Robin made a great Jack, and Sweetums was the perfect giant. At the end, the audience clapped and cheered.

When the curtains closed, Robin jumped into Sweetums' arms. "We made it! We were in the show!"

"And we were pretty good too."

"No job too big or too small, right?" asked Robin.

"Right," said Sweetums.